EMPOWERING STORIES FOR BLACK CHILDREN

Cultivating Confidence,
Kindness and Determination.

By

GOBLEE SMITH

THIS BOOK BELONGS TO

EMPOWERING STORIES FOR BLACK CHILDREN

Goblee Smith

CONTENTS

THE ADVENTURES OF LITTLE BLACK HERO

Once upon a time, there was a little black hero named Marcus. Marcus lived in a small village and was known for his bravery and kind heart.

One day, the village was facing a terrible drought, and the crops were dying. The villagers were getting worried, and they didn't know what to do.

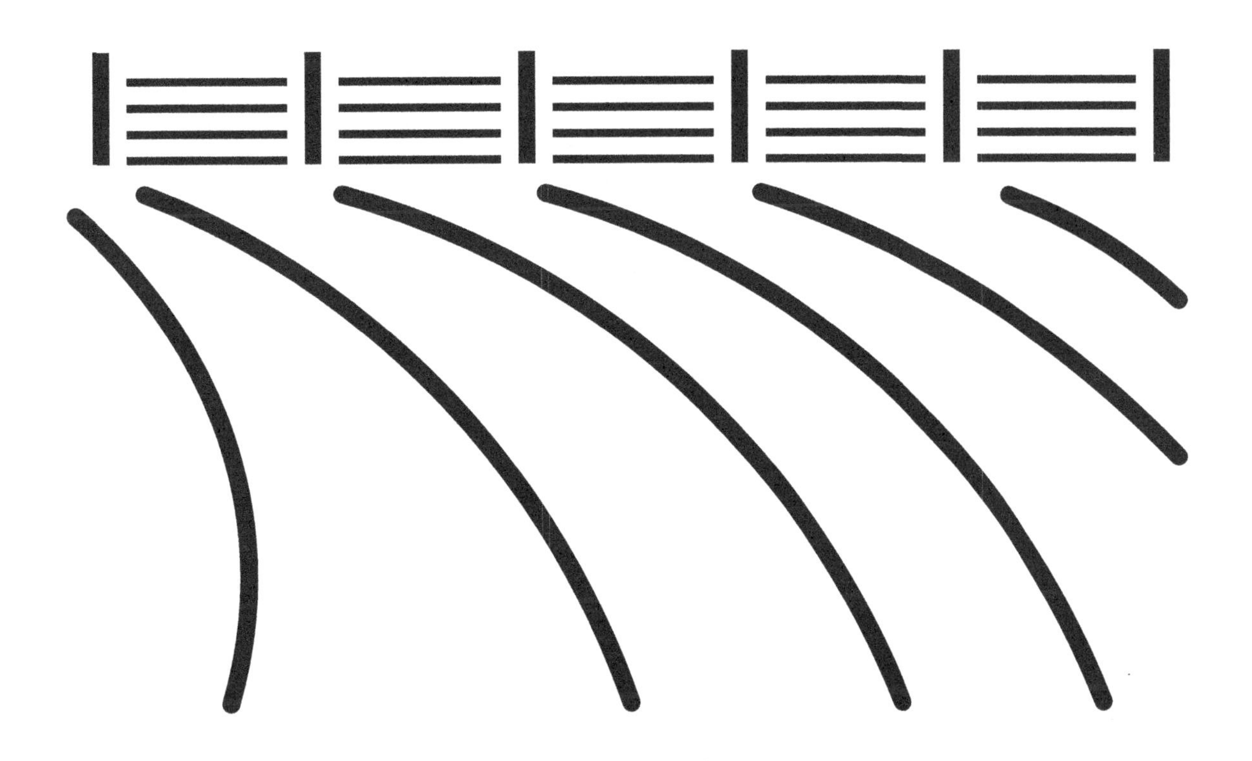

He traveled far and wide, facing many challenges and obstacles along the way.

But he never lost hope and kept pushing forward. Finally, Marcus came across a wise old man who told him about a magic spring that could bring rain to the village.

The old man said that the spring was guarded by a fierce dragon, and only the bravest of heroes could defeat the dragon and bring back the water. Marcus was up for the challenge, and he bravely set out to defeat the dragon.

When he reached the dragon's lair, he was greeted by a massive beast, but he did not let fear take over. Instead, he used his wits and courage to defeat the dragon and retrieve the water from the spring.

Marcus brought the water back to the village, and the villagers were overjoyed. The rain started to fall, and the crops began to grow again. The village was saved, and Marcus was hailed as a hero.

MORAL OF THE STORY

Bravery, determination, and hope can help us overcome even the greatest obstacles. Just like Marcus, we should never give up on our dreams and always believe in ourselves.

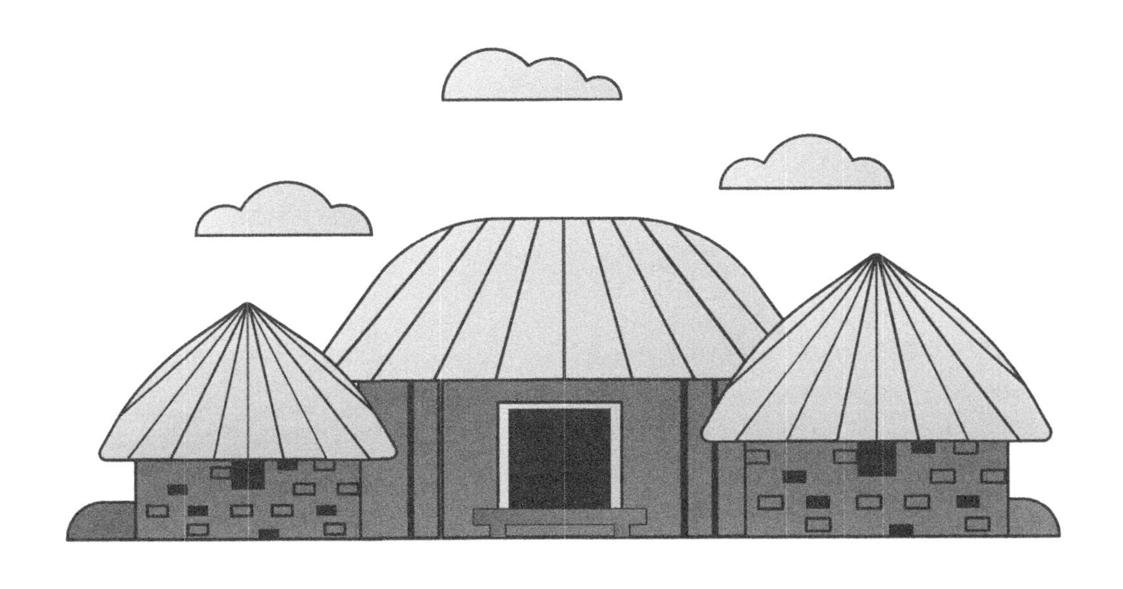

INSPIRATIONAL WORDS

The biggest adventure you can ever take is to live the life of your dreams.

Oprah Winfrey

BLACK IS BEAUTIFUL

Once upon a time, there was a young black girl named Amara. Amara lived in a world where everyone was judged based on their skin color, and black people were often discriminated against.

This made Amara feel self-conscious and sad, as she didn't understand why people couldn't see the beauty in being black. One day, Amara stumbled upon an old book called "Black is Beautiful: A Children's Book."

The book was filled with stories and illustrations of black people from all walks of life, celebrating their unique culture, traditions, and achievements. As Amara read the book, she realized that

being black was something to be proud of. She learned about the rich history of black people and the amazing things they had accomplished, despite facing adversity and discrimination.

From that day on, Amara became a beacon of positivity, spreading the message of "Black is Beautiful" to everyone she met. She inspired others to see the beauty in being black,

and she helped to break down the barriers of discrimination and prejudice.

MORAL OF THE STORY

It's important to embrace our unique qualities and celebrate the things that make us different.

INSPIRATIONAL WORDS

I am the hope of the future. I represent goodness and greatness.

Maya Angelou

BLACK MAGIC: A tale of young wizards

Once upon a time, there was a young black wizard named Elijah. Elijah lived in a world where magic was forbidden, and anyone who practiced it was seen as an outcast. But Elijah had always felt a strong connection to magic, and he knew that he was destined to become a wizard.

Despite the dangers, Elijah refused to give up on his dream. He snuck away from home to study magic in secret, determined to become the best wizard he could be. One day, Elijah was approached by a group of black wizards who called themselves the "Black Magic Circle." They had heard about Elijah's talent and wanted him to join their group.

The Black Magic Circle was dedicated to using their powers for good, and they were determined to change the world and break down the barriers of prejudice and discrimination. Elijah was overjoyed and joined the Black Magic Circle with open arms. Together, they embarked on many adventures, using their magic to help others and bring peace to the world.

However, the world was not ready for a group of black wizards, and they faced many challenges along the way. People were afraid of their powers and sought to destroy them. But Elijah and the Black Magic Circle did not let this defeat them. They stood strong, using their magic to defend themselves and continue their mission of making the world a better place.

MORAL OF THE STORY

We should never give up on our dreams, no matter how difficult the journey may be. Just like Elijah and the Black Magic Circle, we should strive to use our talents and abilities for good and make a positive impact on the world.

INSPIRATIONAL WORDS

Education is the passport to the future, for tomorrow belongs to those who prepare for it today.

Malcolm X

THE MELODIOUS BLACK GIRL

Once upon a time, there was a little black girl named Nia. Nia loved to sing, but she was always too shy to perform in front of others. She was afraid that people would judge her, and she didn't want to make a mistake.

One day, Nia's school announced a talent show, and Nia knew that this was her chance to shine. She had always dreamed of singing on stage, but she was still too afraid to perform. Nia's best friend, a wise old woman, noticed her struggle and offered her some advice. "Nia," she said, "You have a beautiful voice, and the world needs to hear it.

Don't let your fear hold you back. Embrace your talent, and let your voice be heard." Nia took the old woman's words to heart, and she decided to participate in the talent show. She practiced every day, pouring all of her heart and soul into her music. The day of the talent show arrived, and Nia stepped onto the stage.

She was nervous, but she remembered the old woman's words and took a deep breath. And when she started to sing, something magical happened. Her voice filled the room, and she sang with confidence and passion. The audience was mesmerized, and Nia received a standing ovation.

From that day on, Nia became known as the little black girl with the big voice. She continued to pursue her passion for singing, and she inspired others to overcome their fears and embrace their talents.

MORAL OF THE STORY

We should never let our fears hold us back. Just like Nia, we should embrace our passions and talents and let our true selves shine through. With courage and determination, we can accomplish great things and inspire others along the way.

INSPIRATIONAL WORDS

The best way to predict your future is to create it.

Abraham Lincoln

MY BLACK HEROES

Once upon a time, there was a young black boy named Marcus. Marcus lived in a world where black people were often mistreated and discriminated against. He felt frustrated and helpless, as he didn't know how to make a difference.

Marcus decided to organize a march in his city, calling for an end to discrimination and prejudice. He reached out to his friends and neighbors, and together, they began to spread the message of unity and equality. The day of the march arrived, and Marcus was nervous but determined.

The march was peaceful, but powerful, and Marcus' voice echoed through the city, calling for change. The city was moved by Marcus' bravery and determination, and his message of unity and equality inspired others to join the cause. Over time, the community came together, breaking down the barriers of discrimination.

MORAL OF THE STORY

One person can make a difference. Just like Marcus, we should never be afraid to stand up for what is right and fight for change. With courage and determination, we can create a more just and equal world for all.

INSPIRATIONAL WORDS

Success is to be measured not so much by the position that one has reached in life as by the obstacles which he has overcome.

Booker T. Washington

Thank you for choosing to read my book.

As an independent author, your support means the world to me.

If you and your child enjoyed the story, **please consider leaving a review by scanning the QR code.**

Your feedback helps other families discover my work and supports me as a writer.

It only takes 5 seconds to leave a review, and it would mean so much to me.

Thank you again for your support!

- Goblee Smith

Made in the USA
Las Vegas, NV
29 November 2023

81713548R00024